This is for all of us who are adopted, and those who have left space
in their hearts to adopt us back into Indigenous communities, with thanks and lots
of love as we continue to build family and community along the good red road—
kinanâskomitin. —Buffy Sainte-Marie

To all the loves in our lives—the people and creatures and land and water and sky
and stars—and those who we are missing and will see again. For dad, cousin Len,
my son, nieces, sister, and Karen: thank you for your inspiration. —Julie Flett

GLOSSARY

kisâkihitin means "I love you"

kinanâskomitin means "thank you"

kîhtwâm ka-wâpamitonaw means "we'll see each other again"

Greystone Kids / Greystone Books Ltd.
greystonebooks.com

Cataloguing data available from Library and Archives Canada
ISBN 978-1-77164-807-3 (cloth)
ISBN 978-1-77164-808-0 (epub)

Buffy Sainte-Marie is managed by the Paquin Entertainment Group
Editing by Kallie George
Cree language consultation by Solomon Ratt
Copy editing by James Penco
Jacket and interior design by Sara Gillingham Studio
The illustrations in this book were rendered in pastel and pencil, composited digitally.

The author wishes to thank Anthony King for the musical notation.

Printed and bound in China on FSC® certified paper by Shenzhen Reliance Printing.
The FSC® label means that materials used for the product have been responsibly sourced.

Greystone Books thanks the Canada Council for the Arts, the British Columbia Arts Council,
the Province of British Columbia through the Book Publishing Tax Credit,
and the Government of Canada for supporting our publishing activities.

MIX
Paper from
responsible sources
FSC® C102842
www.fsc.org

Canadä

BRITISH
COLUMBIA

BRITISH COLUMBIA
ARTS COUNCIL
An agency of the Province of British Columbia

Canada Council   Conseil des arts
for the Arts   du Canada

Greystone Books gratefully acknowledges the xʷməθkʷəy̓əm (Musqueam),
Sḵwx̱wú7mesh (Squamish), and səlilwətaɬ (Tsleil-Waututh) peoples on
whose land our Vancouver head office is located.

Still
This Love
Goes On

By
**BUFFY
SAINTE-MARIE**

Illustrated by
**JULIE
FLETT**

GREYSTONE KIDS
GREYSTONE BOOKS • VANCOUVER/BERKELEY/LONDON

Sat beside a beaver dam and watched the winter grow.

Ice was hard with little tracks appearing on the snow.

Fog is in the valley now and all the geese have gone.

'Cross the moon I saw them go and . . .

still this love goes on and on.

Still this love goes on.

Once, I saw the summer flowers turn the fields to sun.

Up and down the mountainside, I watched the summer run.

Now the fields are muffled in white and snow is on the dawn.

Morning comes on shivering wings and . . .

still this love goes on and on.

Still this love goes on.

In every dream, I can smell the sweetgrass burning.

And in my heart, I can hear the drum . . .

and hear the singers soaring,

and see the jingle dancers . . .

and still this love goes on and on.

Still this love goes on.

Fancy Dancer come up north to see some friends of his.

Fell in love in a powwow town, and you know how that is.

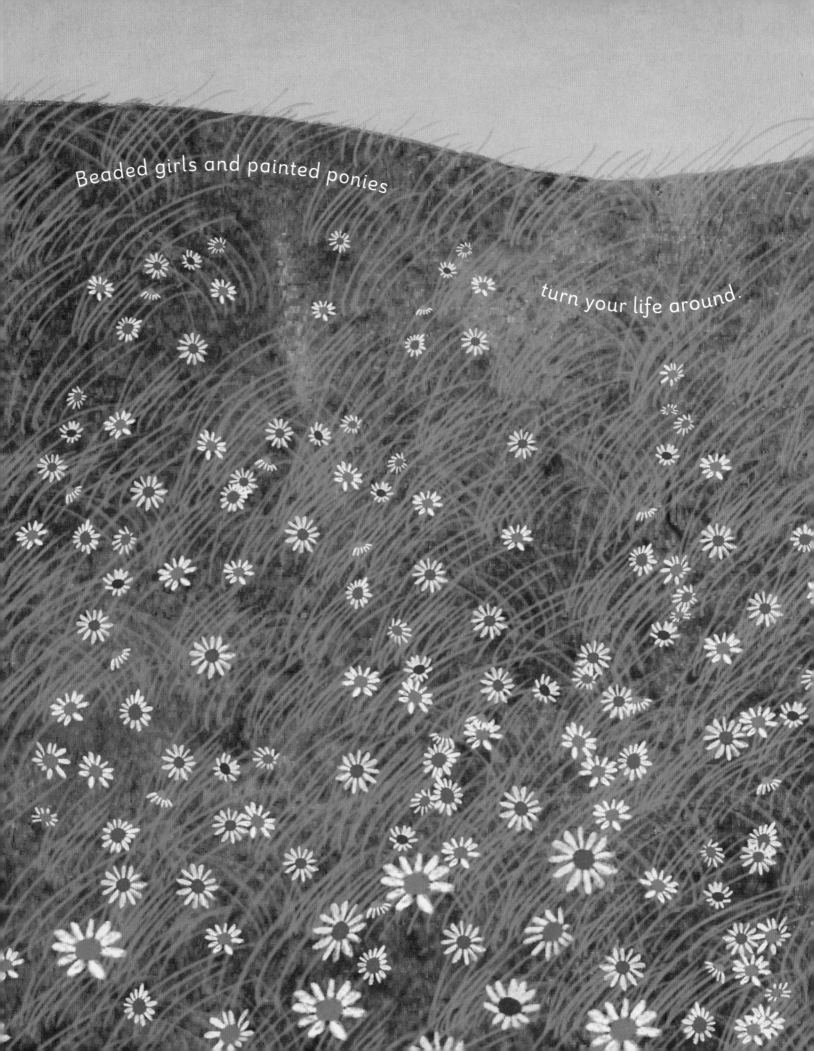

Beaded girls and painted ponies turn your life around.

And now you're singing kisâkihitin, ha ha, on and on . . . .

on and on and on and on and . . .

In every dream, I can smell the sweetgrass burning.

And in my heart, always hear the drum . . .

and hear the singers soaring,

and see the jingle dancers . . .

and still this love goes on and on.

Still this love goes on.

Still This Love Goes On

WORDS AND MUSIC: BUFFY SAINTE-MARIE

Dear Readers and Listeners

I WROTE THIS SONG in a cabin in Alberta, in the wintertime. For me, it was like taking photos with my heart of the things that I see on the reserve. The geese, the ice, the snow, and the people are all there. But I was also thinking about how it is in the other seasons, when everything looks so different. The one thing that stays the same is my love for it all, day after day and year after year—especially the people and our Cree ways, precious like the fragrance of sweetgrass. In Cree, kisâkihitin means "I love you." I hope the words and music inspire you to think about the people and places you love most in your own life. —Buffy

I HAD THE HONOR of working on the pictures for Buffy's beautiful song in Alberta in the winter too! While I was working on the book, I listened to Buffy singing the song at least once a day, if not more. My son and I would hum and sing the lyrics throughout the day, just like all the important songs and music that hold meaning for us; it's imprinted on us now for life. I'm excited to share this song and these pictures with you. I hope that you'll sing and hum along to this beautiful story.

Buffy once said that "Still This Love Goes On" is a happy song, about missing the people who aren't with us. That resonated so deeply with me as I worked on the book, having just moved away from my home of twenty-six years. The lyrics represent a Cree worldview, one in which we don't really have a word for goodbye, but say kîhtwâm ka-wâpamitonaw, which means "we'll see each other again." —Julie